The Princess and The Pumpkin

ADAPTED FROM A MAJORCAN TALE

BY MAGGIE DUFF

PICTURES

BY CATHERINE STOCK

Macmillan Publishing Co., Inc., New York

Collier Macmillan Publishers, London

For Barbara

—M.D.

For Diane

—C.S.

The Princess and the Pumpkin is adapted from a story
in Once There Was and Was Not by B. and G. Dane, illustrated
by Rhea Wells, and is used with permission of Dorothy
Wood, Washington County, Tennessee, Library Board.

Macmillan Publishing Co., Inc.
866 Third Avenue, New York, N.Y. 10022
Collier Macmillan Canada, Ltd.

Printed in the United States of America

10 9 8 7 6 5 4 3 2 1

Library of Congress Cataloging in Publication Data

Duff, Maggie.   The princess and the pumpkin.

"Adapted from a story in Once there was and was not,
by B. and G. Dane."
Summary: An old granny succeeds where others have failed
in curing an ailing princess.
[1. Folklore—Majorca]   I. Stock, Catherine.   II. Title.
PZ8.1.D84Pr   398.2'2'094675 [E]   79-24060   ISBN 0-02-733000-1

2110514

Long ago, in the island town of Palma, there lived a King and Queen who had a daughter. She was the prettiest thing ever, with long golden hair, rosy cheeks, and eyes that sparkled like the morning dew. Now this young and happy Princess loved to dance and sing, and the sound of her laughter rang through the palace like thousands of tiny silver bells.

One warm and sunny day, the Princess was on her balcony with her
ladies-in-waiting. Playing with her kittens, the Princess sang gaily while
the ladies-in-waiting combed her hair with a golden comb. Suddenly,
swoosh!, a flock of green birds flew down from the sky. The leader
seized the golden comb in his beak, and, *swoosh!*, the birds were gone
again. The happy song ceased, and the Princess grew silent.

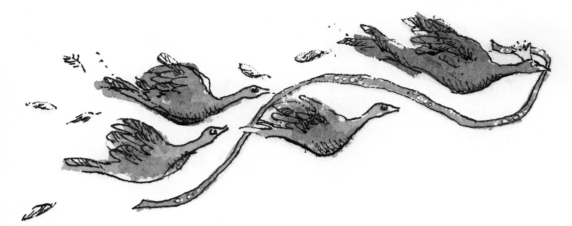

The next day the Princess returned to the balcony with her ladies-in-waiting. As they waited for her dancing master, the ladies braided the Princess's hair and were binding it with an emerald band when, *swoosh!*, the flock of green birds flew down from the sky. The leader seized the emerald band in his beak and, *swoosh!*, the birds were gone again. The happy smile faded from the Princess's face.

The following day was cloudy and gray. The Princess and her ladies-in-waiting sat on the balcony wondering what to do on such a dark, gloomy day. Suddenly, *swoosh!*, the flock of green birds flew down from the sky. The leader snatched a strand of the Princess's golden hair in his beak and, *swoosh!*, the birds were gone. Tears fell from the Princess's eyes and splashed on her hands.

After that, the Princess took to her bed. She refused to eat or to be comforted, and as the days passed she became sadder and sadder and weaker and weaker. The most learned doctors and wisest people in the kingdom were called in, but they could not name the illness or find a cure. At last they decided she must be under an evil spell and declared, "To break the spell and make her well, the Princess must be made to laugh again!"

At once the King decreed that whoever in the kingdom could make the Princess laugh, whether young or old, rich or poor, man or woman, would be kept in comfort forever.

The entire kingdom buzzed with the news. People came in droves to try to make the Princess laugh, for they had nothing to lose and much to gain should they succeed. Some sang, some danced, and some came in costumes. Others told jokes and riddles and tried all sorts of tricks. Children stood on their heads and crossed their eyes while they wiggled their ears. Others came bringing horses dressed in skirts, dogs in bonnets, roosters in trousers, cats in carts, even donkeys wearing feathers. But alas and alack, not even a glimmer of a smile crossed the sad Princess's face, and she grew still weaker.

Then one day when nearly all hope was gone, and it was feared the Princess would die, an old Granny came to town. Now this old Granny's back was bent and her teeth were gone, but her eyes were bright and her step was light and her tongue wagged on and on. When she heard the news about the Princess and the royal decree, she decided right then and there that she would make the dying Princess laugh. "For I would like to be kept in comfort the rest of my days," she told anyone who would listen.

The townspeople laughed. "Don't even try! If the wittiest and wisest in our land cannot make the Princess laugh, how can an old hag like you even hope to succeed? Besides, just one look at you would make the Princess worse! Take our advice—don't waste your time."

"I have as much right as anyone to try," answered the old Granny. "And since I'm not asking to use your legs, what affair of yours is it, anyhow?" With that she turned and left.

The next morning the old Granny was up early. She dressed in her Sunday best and set out for the palace. As she shuffled along, *tris tras, tris tras*, she tried to think of what she might say or do to make the Princess laugh. But try as she would, nothing came to her head worth even a pig's ear.

"Oh dear," she sighed, "what if I should fail like the others? I would not like that at all!" Just then she spied an enormous pumpkin growing in a nearby field.

"Ah! What a pumpkin that is! I will pick it and carry it on my head to the palace. That should make the Princess laugh!"

The old Granny climbed the fence and walked over to the huge pumpkin. Taking hold of it with both hands, she pulled and pulled. But the pumpkin held fast. She pulled even harder. Suddenly the pumpkin broke loose and over she toppled.

She lay there moaning and groaning and calling for help, but none came. At last she thought, "I could lie here till Judgment Day and no one would come to help. And what good would that do the fair Princess? I can never make her laugh if I stay here."

She got up as best she could, dusted herself off, and made sure she had no broken bones. Then she looked around. Where the pumpkin had been, there was now a great gaping hole! She crept to its side and cautiously peered down into it. The hole was so deep she could not see the bottom. Then curiosity took hold and led her down into the hole.

When she finally came up she was chuckling gleefully, her aches and pains forgotten. She carefully covered the hole with sticks and grasses and slowly rolled the pumpkin back into place. Then she was off again for the palace. *Trik, trek.*

As she arrived, Granny found the townspeople still milling about. "Am I too late?" she asked anxiously. "Does the fair Princess still live?"

"The Princess still lives," they answered.

"Has she laughed?" Granny asked.

"The Princess will never laugh," said some.

"Ah then, make way for one who is here to make the Princess laugh," called out the old Granny as she pushed her way through the crowd. They made way all right, for her elbows were sharp in their ribs, but they laughed and jeered as she made her way to the palace gates.

"Such an ugly old hag will never make the Princess laugh," they hooted.

"I am what I am," she answered, "but that does not prevent me from trying."

When she finally reached the King and Queen, they immediately took her to the Princess.

The old Granny bowed very low. "Ah, good day, my Princess, star of my eyes and joy of my heart," she began. "Now you must believe, señorita, when I tell you that as soon as I heard of your strange illness, I came on foot as fast as I could from the far side of this island." The Princess's eyelids fluttered. Then Granny's tongue wagged on and on as she told of finding the enormous pumpkin and how she had discovered the great gaping hole. "And what a bump I got, my Princess, when I toppled over! But it will be well worth it if it makes the fair Princess laugh." She paused.

The Princess stirred, opened her eyes, and then said faintly, "Oh, Granny, tell on, do!"

The old Granny told on. "Now, *señorita*, you must know and believe that when I went down into that hole I found many ladders with gold and silver rungs. I climbed down those ladders until I came to a room filled with tables laden with every good thing to eat you can possibly imagine! I was so hungry and it smelled so good I couldn't resist tasting something. As I reached out for a pastry and a sweet, a terrible voice boomed out, 'Who would take a pastry, and who would take a sweet?'

"'Just a good old Granny who is very hungry,' I answered.

"'A whack on the back and a jab in the ribs for that old Granny. This food is not for her!' the voice shouted.

"Then, my Princess, a silver knife and a silver fork jumped up from the table and started to whack me on the back and jab me in the ribs. Oh, what a whacking and what a jabbing! I can tell you, my Princess, I would have been finished for sure if I had not scrambled out of there in a hurry. And then, how could I have told you this tale?"

A smile played around the Princess's lips, and her eyes began to dance as she spoke in a stronger voice. "Oh, Granny, do tell on!"

"I ran from that room," Granny continued, "and I came into a garden —the most beautiful ever! In the center, a fountain splashed and sparkled in the sun. I sat down to rest. Suddenly, *swoosh!*, down from the sky flew a flock of green birds. They flew right up to the fountain, and as the water splashed on them they turned into handsome young men. The leader was the most handsome of all, but he looked very sad. As he stood there, he took a golden box from his tunic. Reaching into it, he held up, in turn, three glistening objects. Then, sighing, he said,

> This golden comb, this strand of hair,
> Emeralds the Princess once did wear—
> How I wish I'd claimed her hand
> Before this spell fell on the land.
> Now she lies ill, and I have wings
> Until she laughs and claims these things...

"Just then a gust of wind came up, scattering water from the fountain. As it touched the young men, they turned into green birds and flew away.

"And then, *señorita*, my heart was lightened and I laughed with joy, my aches and pains forgotten, for I knew what I must do. I came as fast as I could to tell you this tale, and you must know and must believe, oh my Princess, that every word I have spoken is as true as true can be!"

The Princess sat up, her eyes sparkling. Her smile broke into laughter. She laughed and laughed until she was well and the roses returned to her cheeks.

"Well done, Granny, well done," the Princess said merrily. "Now I must see everything just as you have told it. Let us go at once."

The ladies-in-waiting helped her get dressed while the King and Queen danced for joy. A carriage was ordered, and off they drove.

When they arrived at the field, they ran over to the huge pumpkin and carefully rolled it aside. Quickly they brushed the sticks and grasses away. Sure enough, there was the great gaping hole. Then Granny and the Princess hurried down the gold and silver ladders until they came to the room filled with tables. And sure enough, they were laden with good things to eat.

"Ah, my Princess, do have a pastry and a sweet," coaxed the still hungry Granny.

When the Princess reached out to take them, a voice called out angrily, "Who would take a pastry, and who would take a sweet?"

"The fair Princess of Palma," the old Granny answered.

"Let the Princess take what she will. All is for her," said the voice.

The Princess took a dainty bite of the pastry, then gave the rest to the old Granny, who happily devoured it. Then the Princess nibbled the sweet and gave the rest to Granny, who quickly finished it too.

"Now Granny, do lead on!" said the Princess.

When they reached the garden, it was just as beautiful as Granny had said, and there in the center was the fountain, splashing and sparkling in the sun.

"Let us hide ourselves, my Princess," Granny said, "and see what we will see."

Suddenly, *swoosh!*, out of the sky flew the flock of green birds. Right to the fountain they flew, and as the water splashed on them they turned into handsome young men. The leader took a golden box from his tunic. He reached in and held up a golden comb. *Zas!* A dainty hand darted out from the bushes, snatched the comb, and quickly disappeared.

The young man was startled. He reached into the golden box again, and held up the emerald band. *Zas!* A dainty hand darted out, snatched the band, and again disappeared.

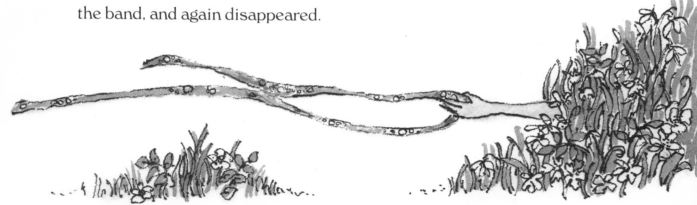

The young man looked puzzled. He slowly reached into the box a third time. Carefully he wound the strand of golden hair around his finger before holding it up. *Zas!* A dainty hand darted out to snatch the golden strand, but this time the handsome young man was ready. He caught the small hand and gently pulled until the beautiful Princess came into view.

"Why did you take these treasures?" he asked wonderingly.

"Because they're mine!" the Princess answered.

"Ah! Then you are my true love and have broken the wicked spell. We are free! Fair Princess, will you marry me?"

"Gladly," she answered, for she liked what she saw, "providing my parents agree. You can ask now, for they await us at the top."

So with Granny leading the way, they climbed out of the hole. The Prince, for that was what he was, fell to his knees before the King and Queen and asked for the Princess's hand in marriage. Quite overcome by all that had happened, they gave their consent at once. Then all returned to the palace and the festivities began without delay. The wedding celebration lasted for days and days, with each day's entertainment better than the one before. And after that the Prince and Princess lived together happily for many years.

As for the old Granny, true to the royal decree, she was kept in comfort for the rest of her days. And whenever foreign dignitaries came to court, she gladly told her story to anyone who would listen.

And now you must know and must believe, it's all as true as true can be!